VISIT US AT
www.abdopublishing.com

Reinforced library bound edition published in 2010 by Spotlight, a division of the ABDO Group, 8000 West 78th Street, Edina, Minnesota 55439. Spotlight produces high-quality reinforced library bound editions for schools and libraries. Published by agreement with Warner Bros.—A Time Warner Company. All rights reserved. Used under authorization.

Printed in the United States of America, North Mankato, Minnesota.
092009
012011

 PRINTED ON RECYCLED PAPER

Library of Congress Cataloging-in-Publication Data

Fisch, Sholly.
  Scooby-Doo in Trick or treat! / writer, Sholly Fisch ; penciller, Joe Staton ; inker, Scott McRae ; colorist, Heroic Age ; letterer, Mike Sellers. -- Reinforced library bound ed.
     p. cm. -- (Scooby-Doo graphic novels)
  ISBN 978-1-59961-699-5
  1. Graphic novels. I. Staton, Joe. II. Scooby-Doo (Television program) III. Title. IV. Title: Trick or treat!
  PZ7.7.F57Sc 2010
  741.5'973--dc22

                                2009032904

All Spotlight books have reinforced library bindings and
are manufactured in the United States of America.

SCOOBY'S MINI-MYSTERIES
FLY BY NIGHT

CAN YOU SOLVE IT BEFORE SCOOBY AND THE GANG?

SHOLLY FISCH — STORY
JOB STATON — PENCILS
SCOTT MCRAE — INKS
HEROIC AGE — COLORS
MIKE SELLERS — LETTERS
JEANINE SCHAEFER — EDITOR

TAKE ACTION *NOW*, PEOPLE, BEFORE IT'S *TOO LATE!*

THE ALIENS ARE COMING!

R-RALIENS?

THOSE *BUG-EYED INVADERS* ARE ON THEIR WAY TO STEAL YOUR *HOMES*, YOUR *LUNCH*, AND YOUR *BRAINS!*

ARE *YOU* PREPARED TO DEFEND YOURSELVES?

OUR *LUNCH?!* ZOINKS!

WHAT CAN WE DO?

YOU'RE *IN LUCK*, MY FRIEND! I HAVE HERE THE LATEST HI-TECH, *ANTI-ALIEN TECHNOLOGY*, STRAIGHT FROM THE SCIENTISTS AT THE *PENTAGON!*

FOR ONLY *FIFTY DOLLARS*, THIS LIFE-SAVING EQUIPMENT CAN BE YOURS!

E.T. B-GONE
ANTI-ALIEN DEFENSE SYSTEM
AS SEEN ON PUBLIC ACCESS TV

AW, COME ON! DO YOU *REALLY* THINK ALIENS WOULD COME *HERE?*

I DON'T JUST *THINK* IT! I HAVE *CONCRETE EVIDENCE* THAT THEY'RE ALREADY *HERE!*

LOOK AT THESE PHOTOS OF *FLYING SAUCERS* FLYING RIGHT OVER *YOUR TOWN HALL!*

I'LL BUY ONE OF THOSE!

SIGN ME UP!

WHOA! SAVE YOUR *MONEY*, FOLKS! THOSE PHOTOS ARE *FAKES!*

DON'T BE *RIDICULOUS! PICTURES DON'T LIE!*

WELL, *THESE* PICTURES LIE --

-- AND I CAN *PROVE* IT!

DID YOU SPOT VELMA'S PROOF? TAKE ANOTHER LOOK AND SEE IF YOU CAN FIND IT. THEN TURN TO THE END OF THIS ISSUE TO CHECK IF YOU'RE RIGHT!

GHOSTS IN THE MYSTERY MACHINE

Robbie Busch
Story

Karen Matchette
Art

Heroic Age
Colors

Mike Sellers
Letters

Jeanine Schaefer
Editor

...AND FINALLY, *CHOO CHOO* WILL DEAL WITH RIPPING OUT THE OLD SEATS AND PUTTING IN SOME STATE OF THE ART ASTRO-PLEATHER THAT WILL CONFORM TO YOUR BODIES ON LONG STAKEOUTS.

IT'S LIKE *BUTTAH!*

KILLER! I'M SO GLAD YOU DECIDED TO TAKE OVER YOUR POP'S BUSINESS AFTER YOU FINISHED YOUR CRIMINOLOGY DEGREE!

LIKE, WE'LL LET YOU GUYS GET TO IT.

REE RA RATER. RIME ROR *ROOBY RACKS!*

HA! NO SWEAT, SCOOB. I KNOW HOW YOU NEED YOUR *SNACKS!*

YO, X! CHECK THIS OUT!

HMM... THAT'S *WEIRD.* I DON'T SEE THAT ON THE *OLD BLUE-PRINTS.*

MAYBE IT'S SOMETHING YOUR *POP* PUT IN THERE.

PERHAPS, *POP* HAD SOME REAL *TRICKS* UP HIS SLEEVE... *WHOA!*

VZZZZROO

HELLO... XAVIER... DO YOU WANT TO PLAY A *GAME?*

HOW'D'YA KNOW MY *NAME?!* I'M NOT INTO THAT *WAR GAMES* SCENE!

AAAAAHHHH!

THE END

A WELL-LAID TRAP

JOHN ROZUM
STORY

VINCE DEPORTER
ART

HEROIC AGE
COLORS

MIKE SELLERS
LETTERS

JEANINE SCHAEFER
EDITOR

LOOK! THE SEA HEAP IS GETTING AWAY!

HE'S MORE SLIPPERY THAN HE SEEMS, BUT THIS NET OUGHT TO CATCH HIM.

THAT'S A GREAT TRAP, FREDDIE, BUT WHAT ARE YOU GOING TO USE FOR BAIT?

WHAT ABOUT THESE MOSTESS FRUIT PIES?

THEY COME IN THREE DIFFERENT FLAVORS THAT NO MONSTER CAN RESIST: BLUEBERRY, CHERRY, AND APPLE.

JINKIES! THAT WAS FAST!

BUT WE STILL DON'T HAVE OUR MONSTER. LOOK!

LIKE, WE COULDN'T RESIST THEM EITHER. THE TENDER, FLAKY CRUST...

REAL ROOT RILLING. RELICIOUS!

DARN! THAT TRAP AND THOSE DELICIOUS MOSTESS FRUIT PIES WOULD HAVE BEEN MINE IF IT WEREN'T FOR THOSE MEDDLING KIDS.

EVERY BITE IS OUT OF SIGHT WITH MOSTESS FRUIT PIES

ZOINKS! THE GHOST DISAPPEARED INTO *THIN AIR!*

OR MAYBE INTO THAT *DOOR!* COME ON!

IT LOOKS LIKE A *CLOCK ST--*

AAAGH!

BING

BONG

DING

DONG

CLANG

EXCUSE ME. DID A *GHOST* RUN THROUGH HERE?

WHAT DID YOU SAY? I'VE GOT THIS, LIKE, *RINGING IN MY EARS...*

A GHOST? YEAH, SURE -- RIGHT BETWEEN THE *FAIRY* AND *LEPRECHAUN.*

NO, NO ONE'S BEEN THROUGH HERE IN THE PAST *HOUR.*

IT CAN'T BE! THIS IS THE *ONLY* PLACE THE GHOST COULD HAVE GONE.

HMM. MAYBE *HE'S* THE GHOST. BUT WHERE COULD HE HAVE STASHED HIS *COSTUME* AND THE *JEWELS?*

I THINK *I* KNOW!

WHERE ARE THE COSTUME AND JEWELS? GO BACK AND SEE IF YOU CAN SPOT THE TELLTALE CLUE. THEN TURN TO THE BACK OF THIS ISSUE AND CHECK YOUR ANSWER!

MONSTER MIX-UP

ROBBIE BUSCH
STORY

VINCE DEPORTER
PENCILS

**VINCE DEPORTER
& DAN DAVIS**
INKS

HEROIC AGE
COLORS

MIKE SELLERS
LETTERS

JEANINE SCHAEFER
EDITOR

SHAGGY! SCOOBY! *FOLLOW ME!*

BUT THAT'S THE WAY THE MONSTER WENT! WHY DON'T WE DO SOMETHING DIFFERENT THIS TIME LIKE...

RUN THE OTHER WAY?!

RAAWRR?!

ROINKS!

WHATCHA WAITIN' FOR, VELMA?! *RUN!!!*

THAT'S THE *SPIRIT!*

WHOOSH

NOW THERE'S *SPIRITS* TOO?! LET'S NOT CHECK THE *BATHTUB.* I BET THE *LOCH NESS MONSTER* IS IN THERE!!!

LET'S CORNER THAT OTHER MONSTER *UPSTAIRS!*

OKAY!

AARRROO!!!

SLAM!

UGH! THAT'S NOT VERY HOSPITABLE!

OOF! LET'S SHOW HIM A LITTLE MYSTERY INC. MANNERS!

GAARRRFFF!

WHOA!

NOW HE'S *TRAPPED!*

YOU CALL THAT TRAPPED? HE'S IN THERE WITH ALL OF THE *FOOD!*

MMM...RI RALL RAT *RACATION!*

MMWAAARGH!

BAM!

JINKIES! THAT'S THE *WRONG* MONSTER!

RHO RARES...*RUN!*

HEY! THE MONSTERS...

...SWITCHED PLACES!

STOP!

LIKE, JACKKNIFED *MYSTERY INC.* ON THE TERROR TURNPIKE! OOOOF!

THERE MUST BE A *SECRET PASSAGEWAY* BETWEEN HERE AND THE UPSTAIRS!

I THINK I UNDERSTAND, VELMA. AND WE CAN *CATCH* THEM AT THEIR OWN *GAME!*

MMM... THEN HOW DID THE MONSTERS *SWITCH*...CRUNCH... *PLACES?*

I'M NOT SO SURE...

I HOPE THIS *WORKS!* TRY TO BE A LITTLE QUIETER ON THE STAIRS.

SQUEEK SQUEEK

KLOMP

GRRRRRR!!!

WHAT?

RUUUUN!

IIIEEEE!!

HA HA HA!!!

BWAAGGGHH!

QUICK! IN HERE!

COMING!

AAAAHHHHH!

YAARRGHH! HA HA HA!

WHA?! YIPES!

NOW WE'VE GOT YOU!

THANKS, VELMA!

LOOK OUT! THOSE *KIDS* ARE...

...VAMPIRES! OOOOF!

BLAM-O

GOOD PLAN, VELMA!

SO THEY WERE EACH WEARING BOTH COSTUMES!

THAT'S HOW THEY COULD CHANGE TO THE OTHER MONSTER SO QUICKLY!

WELL, YOUR *VAMPIRE* MAKE-UP REALLY HELPED TAKE A *BITE* OUT OF THEIR PLANS, DAPHNE!

LIKE, NOW LET'S TAKE A BITE OUT OF A SCOOBY SNACK!

ROOBY-ROOBY-ROOOOO!

THE END

VELMA'S MONSTERS OF THE WORLD: WEREWOLVES

JOHN ROZUM: STORY
DAN DAVIS: ART
HEROIC AGE: COLORS
MIKE SELLERS: LETTERS
JEANINE SCHAEFER: EDITOR

HELLO, EVERYONE. THANKS FOR JOINING ME.

TODAY WE ARE GOING TO BE TALKING ABOUT WEREWOLVES!

WERE-WOLVES

"THE WORD "WEREWOLF" ACTUALLY MEANS "MAN-WOLF," A PERSON WHO UNDER CERTAIN CONDITIONS CAN *TRANSFORM* HIMSELF INTO A WOLF.

"THIS IS A VERY OLD BELIEF THAT BELONGS TO DIFFERENT CULTURES ALL OVER THE WORLD."

"WOLVES AREN'T THE ONLY ANIMALS THAT PEOPLE WERE BELIEVED TO CHANGE INTO. NEW GUINEA HAD *WERE-CROCODILES*, EUROPE HAD *WERE-BEARS*, INDIA HAD *WERE-TIGERS*, AND AFRICA HAD *LEOPARD-MEN* AND *HYENA-MEN*."

SO, HOW DOES A PERSON *TRANSFORM* INTO AN *ANIMAL*? WELL, *GODS* COULD DO IT AT *WILL*, BUT FOR *NORMAL*, MORTAL *PEOPLE*, THERE WERE A *NUMBER OF WAYS.*

IN SOME CASES, A PERSON WOULD *BREAK A SACRED LAW*, AND BE TURNED INTO A WOLF AS *PUNISHMENT. CURSES* COULD TURN INNOCENT PEOPLE OR CRIMINALS INTO WOLVES, USUALLY FOR PERIODS OF *SEVERAL YEARS.*

"ACCORDING TO GREEK *MYTH*, KING LYCAEON *ANGERED* THE GOD *ZEUS*, AND WAS *TRANSFORMED* INTO A WOLF AS *PUNISHMENT.*

"THIS GAVE US THE WORD '*LYCANTHROPE*,' THE TECHNICAL TERM FOR A WEREWOLF.

"ACCORDING TO SOME, *SLEEPING OUTDOORS* UNDER A *FULL MOON* ON A FRIDAY NIGHT WILL DO IT. FULL MOONS ARE OFTEN ASSOCIATED WITH WEREWOLVES, BUT MOSTLY IN THE MOVIES.

"OTHERS SAY THAT *DRINKING WATER* FROM A *WOLF'S FOOTPRINT* OR FROM A *STREAM* WHERE A WOLF PACK HAS DRUNK WILL CAUSE THE PERSON TO CHANGE.

"PEOPLE WITH *CONNECTING EYEBROWS*, *POINTY EARS* AND *RING* FINGERS AS LONG AS THEIR MIDDLE FINGERS WERE THOUGHT TO BE WEREWOLVES.

"DURING THE *RENAISSANCE*, TRANSFORMATION BECAME ASSOCIATED WITH WITCHES WHO WERE BELIEVED TO BE ABLE TO TURN INTO CATS, HARES, AND TOADS."

SOMETIMES, IT WAS SIMPLY BECAUSE YOUR *ANCESTORS* COULD DO IT, BUT THE MOST *COMMON* METHOD OF TRANSFORMATION WAS *EITHER* THROUGH *MAGIC* CHARMS, SALVES, SPELLS, AND RITUALS, OR...

"...BY *PUTTING ON THE SKIN* OF A WOLF, OR A WOLF *MASK*, AND *BEHAVING LIKE* THE ANIMAL.

"SOMETIMES *ALL* IT TAKES IS A *BELT* MADE FROM THE SKIN OF THAT ANIMAL.

"*UNLIKE* WHAT YOU SEE IN THE *MOVIES*, IT WAS RARE FOR WEREWOLVES OF LEGEND TO BE AT ALL *MAN-LIKE* IN APPEARANCE.

"IN THE MIDDLE AGES, AN EXCESSIVELY *HAIRY* MAN CLAIMING TO BE A WEREWOLF WOULD BE VIEWED AS BEING A BIT OF A *NUT.*"

DO YOU **WANT** TO **SEE** A MAN TURN INTO A **WOLF?** JUST **REARRANGE** THE PANELS BELOW INTO THE **CORRECT ORDER.**

MOST LEGENDS **AGREE** THAT THE WOLF **AUTOMATICALLY** TURNS BACK INTO A PERSON DURING THE **DAY,** OR WHEN THEY ARE KILLED.

SOMETIMES **MAGIC** IS NECESSARY, BUT OFTEN YOU CAN **STOP** A WEREWOLF WITH ORDINARY **WEAPONS.** SILVER BULLETS ARE THE INVENTION OF THE MOVIES. SOMETIMES, ALL YOU **NEED** TO DO IS CALL OUT THEIR HUMAN **NAME,** AND THEY'LL TURN BACK INTO A PERSON.

BUT, **I FIND** THAT THE **BEST** WAY TO TURN A WEREWOLF BACK INTO A MAN IS SIMPLY TO PULL OFF HIS **MASK.**

GRMBLE MUTTER GRMP.

THE END

SCOOBY'S MINI-MYSTERIES

SOLUTION PAGE:
FLY BY NIGHT & TIME TO SCARE

SHOLLY FISCH
STORY

JOE STATON
PENCILS

SCOTT McRAE
INKS

HEROIC AGE
COLORS

MIKE SELLERS
LETTERS

JEANINE SCHAEFER
EDITOR

SEE? THE SHADOWS ON TOWN HALL FACE ONE WAY, BUT THE SHADOWS ON THE UFOS GO IN THE *OPPOSITE* DIRECTION.

THAT MEANS YOU FAKED THE PHOTO -- BY COMBINING TWO DIFFERENT PICTURES!

BUT DON'T WORRY! I BET THESE PEOPLE WOULD BE GLAD TO SEND YOU INTO *OUTER SPACE!*

THE END

STOP

DON'T KEEP READING! FIRST, TURN BACK AND READ THE STORY CALLED *"TIME TO SCARE."* THEN COME BACK HERE TO CHECK YOUR ANSWER!

CHECK IT OUT! ALL OF THE CLOCKS SHOW THE SAME TIME -- EXCEPT *THIS* ONE!

I'D GUESS SOMEONE *STOPPED* THIS CLOCK FOR A FEW MINUTES, TO PUT SOMETHING *INSIDE.*

BAH! I COULD'VE *GOTTEN AWAY* WITH IT IF I HAD *TWO MINUTES* TO RESET THE CLOCK!

NO PROBLEM! WHERE YOU'RE GOING, YOU'LL HAVE PLENTY OF TIME!

YEAH, LIKE *FIFTEEN TO TWENTY YEARS!*

THE END